For Vincent and Ian
B.T.

First American edition published in 2007
by Boxer Books Limited.

Distributed in the United States and Canada by
Sterling Publishing Co., Inc.
387 Park Avenue South, New York, NY 10016-8810

First published in Great Britain in 2007
by Boxer Books Limited.
www.boxerbooks.com

Text and illustrations copyright © 2007 Britta Teckentrup

The rights of Britta Teckentrup to be identified as the author
and illustrator of this work have been asserted by her
in accordance with the Copyright, Designs and Patents Act, 1988.

ISBN-13: 978-1-905417-37-7
ISBN-10: 1-905417-37-3

1 3 5 7 9 10 8 6 4 2

Printed in China

Big Smelly Bear

Britta Teckentrup

Boxer Books

Big Smelly Bear never washed.

Big Smelly Bear never brushed.

Big Smelly Bear never took a bath.

Big Smelly Bear was followed
by a big smelly stink wherever he went.

Flies buzzed all around him.

But they were the only ones that ever
came close.

When the animals in the forest got a whiff of Big Smelly Bear, they ran away as quickly as they could.

None of this seemed to bother Big Smelly Bear. But sometimes he did think that it would be nice to have a friend.

Then, one morning, everything changed.

Big Smelly Bear woke up with the most terrible itch. He tried to scratch his back with his paw... but he couldn't reach.

He tried rolling on the ground in the dirt.
But that didn't stop the itching either.
Big Smelly Bear was itchier
and dustier than ever.

He tried scratching his back
with a tree branch.
But that made the itch even itchier.

He tried rubbing his back against
the trunk of an old tree.
But that didn't help at all.

"I would scratch your back for you,"
said a voice from above,
"but you are much too smelly."

Big Smelly Bear looked up and saw
a Big Fluffy Bear sitting in some branches.
Big Fluffy Bear smiled at Big Smelly Bear.

"Why don't you take a bath?" asked Big Fluffy Bear. "Then you wouldn't itch *or* smell."

"Because I don't need a bath," replied Big Smelly Bear.

"Yes, you do," said Big Fluffy Bear.

"No, I don't!" said Big Smelly Bear.

"YES, you do!" growled Big Fluffy Bear.

"NO, I DO NOT!" growled Big Smelly Bear back.

"YES, YOU DO!" cried Big Fluffy Bear.

"NO, I DO NOT!" shouted Big Smelly Bear.

"Yes you do!"

shouted Big Fluffy Bear.

"Because you stink!"

Both big bears sat quietly for a minute.
Then Big Smelly Bear sighed a big sigh.
"Oh, all right!" he said, and he stomped off
grumpily down the hill to the pond.

When Big Smelly Bear got out of the pond,
he shook the water from his big body.

Big Fluffy Bear jumped down from the tree and sniffed.
"There," she said, "that's much better. Now you smell
all clean."And she scratched his back for him.

The itch was gone!

Big Smelly Bear sighed.

"Thank you," he said.

Then he gave Big Fluffy Bear's back
a little scratch, too.

"I'm not going to take any more baths,"
said Big Smelly Bear.

Big Fluffy Bear smiled, and the two
big bears had a little bear hug.

Big Smelly Bear liked Big Fluffy Bear very much.
Even though he said he would never bathe again,
sometimes, late at night, he would wander down
to the big pond.

And can you guess what he was doing?